Smart Dog

Published by Caroline House

Boyds Mills Press, Inc.

A Highlights Company

910 Church Street

Honesdale, Pennsylvania 18431

Publisher Cataloging-in-Publication Data

Leemis, Ralph.

Smart dog / by Ralph Leemis ; illustrated by Chris L. Demarest.

—1st ed.

[32] p. : col. ill. ; cm.

Summary: A farmer dreams of what his life might be like if his dog were a celebrity, only to discover that he likes his life just the way it is.

ISBN 1-56397-109-7

1. Dogs—Juvenile fiction. [1. Dogs—Fiction.] I. Demarest, Chris L., ill.
II. Title.   [E]—dc20   1993

Library of Congress Catalog

Card Number: 92-71274

First edition, 1993

Book designed by Joy Chu

The text of this book is set in 18-point Cochin.

The illustrations are done in watercolors.

Distributed by St. Martin's Press

Printed in the United States of America

10 9 8 7 6 5 4 3 2 1

SMART DOG

by Ralph Leemis
Illustrated by Chris L. Demarest

CAROLINE HOUSE / BOYDS MILLS PRESS

"If you were a smart dog, you'd chase that rabbit."

"Or do something, not just lie here all day."

"If you were a smart dog, you would learn a new trick—like roll over, play dead, or beg for a treat."

"If you were a smart dog, you'd stand on your hind legs, and I'd play my fiddle for coins in the street."

"You'd wear bells on your tail and dance on a drum.
People would come to watch the one-dog band."

"And when you got better, we'd travel around. Folks would pay money to see you dance on the keys."

"Then, while you conducted your own string quartet,

the crowd would applaud as you juggled."

"We would have money, a car with a driver . . ."

"to take us through town at the head of parades."

"And there would be movies, with you as the hero.
The people would love us, as you saved the day."

"Then as you grew smarter, there'd be public speeches . . ."

"and every night filming for national shows."

"Our lives would be busy, with hustle and bustle."

"But we'd save our money, because
you're smart that way."

"Some day we'd retire, and life would be easy."

"We'd buy a small house in the country for two."

"I guess you're smarter than I thought."